You, Me and Thing:

The Legend of the Loch Ness Lilo

You, me and Thing

Karen McCombie

Illustrated by Alex T. Smith

ff

faber and faber

First published in 2012
by Faber and Faber Limited
Bloomsbury House,
74–77 Great Russell Street,
London, WC1B 3DA

Typeset by Faber and Faber
Printed in England by CPI Group (UK) Ltd, Croydon, CR0 4YY

A CIP record for this book
is available from the British Library

ISBN 978–0–571–27261–7

2 4 6 8 10 9 7 5 3 1

For Weezy (woo!)
and Tom (Tom)

Contents

A thing called Thing

Think of a thing.

Quite a *small* sort of thing.

A thing that's covered in ginger fur, like a red squirrel.

Now *stop* thinking about red squirrels, because it's *not* one of those.

Think of paws that are a little bit like hands.

Think of wings that are stubby and don't work.

Think of two HUGE eyes that blink up at

you, all shy and wondering and worried.

'Hmm. What sort of thing *is* this funny little thing?' you might ask.

Well, it's *my* thing. Mine and Jackson's.

Our thing lives—

'Hold on . . . wait a minute,' you might interrupt. '*Who* is *Jackson*?'

Well, he is:

- my neighbour (in the new house next door to my old cottage)

- nine years old (same as me)

- my friend (a lot of the time), and

- very annoying (even **MORE** of the time).

When I first met Jackson Miller, I liked

Jackson!

him about as much as I like stepping on slugs in bare feet.

But then we accidentally discovered the strange small something hiding in the scraggle of trees between our back gardens and the sprawling new housing estate beyond it.

That strange small something changed *everything*.

Suddenly, out-sneering each other wasn't

top of our list of things to do – not when we had a secret *all* to ourselves.

That's right; it's a secret not even our mums and dads know about.

Though the way me and Jackson see it, it's not as if we tell them any *lies* exactly.

sssh!

Most days after school, I'll say, 'I'm going to hang out with Jackson.' At the same time, Jackson will say, 'I'm going to hang out with Ruby.'

I guess our parents think we're scampering off to climb the trees and make dens in the roots and chat about this and that and all sorts.

Well, that's one hundred per cent true, of course.

We just leave out the bit about the weird sort of squirrel/troll/fairy which is hanging out *with* us . . .

'Ooh! Can you tell us *more* about your

strange, um, thing?' I hear you ask.

Sure.

Here goes.

Our thing . . .

- is called Thing.

- used to live deep in the middle of Muir Wood, before it got chopped down and built over.

- can do **MAGIC**.

That last bit sounds exciting, doesn't it?

The trouble is, Thing doesn't seem to be able to do *good* or *useful* magic, like turning Brussels sprouts into cupcakes or whatever.

Thing's magic tends to get muddled and troublesome.

I mean, you should have *seen* what it did at the leisure centre pool last week.

One little kid saw, for sure.

I bet he'll remember it his whole life.

I bet he'll be telling his grandchildren all about the Legend of the Loch Ness Lilo in sixty years' time.

Me? Well, I just want to forget all about it.

And I will, *right* after I tell you what happened . . .

Happy birdie?

'Wheeeee!'

Thing seemed to be as happy as a Thing can be on a sunny Monday afternoon.

'Wahhhh!' it squeaked, as it boinged on the mini trampoline we'd made.

It's amazing what you can do with a cake tin and a stretched red rubber swimming cap.

But ever since we found Thing, me and Jackson have tried hard to make it feel at home here in this little patch of trees, which is all that's left of the forest.

In fact, while Thing was boinging, *I* was busy making a daisy chain to hang around the entrance of its cosy home.

(Thing's cosy home is an old Scooby-Doo Mystery Machine van, kindly donated by Jackson, and hidden under twigs and ferns.)

And Jackson had just sneaked a plastic tub from his kitchen, so Thing had somewhere to store its two favourite foods.

(Mushrooms and jelly babies, if you were wondering.)

As I draped the daisy chain over the open back doors, Thing bounced, boinged and called out 'I *loves* trampling!!' in its funny, purry voice.

Oh.

Didn't I mention it can talk?

No? Well, it can.

Thing speaks our language, *and* other

languages. (It taught me and Jackson a rude word in pigeon the other day.)

'Have fun trampling *now*,' said Jackson, tossing an orange jelly baby in the air and catching it expertly in his mouth, ''cause Ruby's going to need her swimming cap back at the weekend!'

The wheeing and the boinging immediately stopped.

'Rubby?' Thing said questioningly.

(It has never learned to say my name
properly.)

'Yes?' I replied, noticing that Thing was
anxiously rubbing its little paws/hands
together and rocking from side to side.

'What Boy *meaninging*?'

(It's never learned Jackson's name at *all*.)

'Don't listen to him – I won't spoil your
trampoline,' I said quickly, not wanting
Thing to worry. 'I told Mum I ripped that
cap and she bought me a new one.'

Worrying isn't good for Thing, *or* for us.
It's often what sets off the rubbish magic.

'Nice one!' said Jackson, admiring my fib

as he tossed a second jelly baby into the air. 'Can't *wait* for Saturday. Can you?'

'Where is *you* and Boy doing on Sat-urrrr-day?' Thing asked.

'Well,' I began, 'we've been invited to—'

'—a pool party!' Jackson barged in and answered for me.

'What is *poo* party?' asked Thing, all curiosity and puppy-dog eyes.

'FTTT-NUHH-GIHUHH!' Jackson snorted, sniggering and choking on his jelly baby.

'He means it's a birthday party. At the local swimming pool,' I said quickly, whacking Jackson nice and *hard* on the back.

I hoped the whack might stop him choking, AND let him know he should SHUT UP.

'Cause Thing does *not* like to be teased.

It makes it nervous.

And quite possibly cross.

Even just a little bit *ARRGHH!*

And if Thing feels *ARRGHH!*,

rubbish magic is *definitely* only a

crackle, spit and *fizzzzzzzzzz*

away . . .

Luckily, Thing hadn't noticed

Jackson acting like a dumb donut.

'Birdie party sound *nice!*' it purred,

looking up into the springy branches

above us.

Sigh.

Sometimes, trying to explain

the world to Thing can twist your

thoughts up in knots.

'Er, no . . . there won't be any birds,' I said, imagining the Dolphin Leisure Centre all a-flutter with starlings and sparrows in tiny party hats and with tooters.

'This boy Ali in our class – it's *his* party, and the whole class is invited!' Jackson jumped in, now that he'd got his breath back. 'First we go swimming, and then we eat crisps and ice-cream!'

'What is *zwimmin*, Rubby?' Thing blinked at me.

'Look! It's when you jump into water and do *this*,' said Jackson miming a front crawl.

Bad idea – it made the last of the jelly babies spill out of the packet he was clutching.

Puzzled or not, Thing wasn't about to pass up the chance of a stray sweet or two. It hopped off its homemade trampoline and picked the nearest one up off the scrubby ground.

'Why?' it asked, biting the head off a yellow jelly baby.

'Why what?' Jackson asked back.

'Why *waving* in wet? Why?' Thing blinked, just as confused.

OK, so swimming and pools might be hard to describe to a small weird something that's lived in a deep dark wood for the whole of its odd little life.

'Well . . .' I began uncertainly, scrabbling in my mind for words that might work.

'*I* know!' said Jackson, suddenly smiling one of his big baboon grins (uh-oh). 'We *could* always take Thing along with us on Saturday! I'll wrap it in a really big towel and—'

'Nope!' I cut him off quickly.

I knew Jackson had a large, roomy space in his head where his brain should be, but had he already forgotten what happened the time we sneaked Thing into school?

We **NEARLY** got into a truckload of trouble.

Thanks to a wonky spell of Thing's, the soggy noodles for lunch came alive and doodled around the dinner hall!

If we (and the noodle-doodles) had been caught . . .

'Aw, go on, Ruby!' Jackson began pleading. 'We'd be careful this time, and . . .'

While Jackson babbled, I spotted something.

A furry something called Christine, who happens to be my extremely ancient cat.

Christine cat was sitting under the old stone birdbath, watching blue tits splish-sploshing above her.

As she twitched stray drips and droplets from her whiskers, I had an idea.

An idea of a way that I could explain 'zwimmin' and pools to Thing. (Which was going to be a whole lot easier and safer than sneaking Thing into the leisure centre, *that's* for sure.)

'Come here,' I said, ignoring Jackson and scooping up Thing.

I peeked over the top of the low stone wall to check for any random parents.

Nope – all clear.

'OK. See that little blue tit? The one splashing around?' I whispered, and pointed towards the birdbath.

Thing scuttled out of my arms and up on to my shoulder for a better view.

'Yes, *please*, Rubby,' it whis-*purr*ed.

'It looks like it's having fun, doesn't it?' I said, as the bird dipped its beak down, tilted

its head back and shook a shower of water
all over itself.

'Yes, *please*, Rubby,' Thing repeated.

'Well, imagine a big, big room, with the
floor all filled with water –'

Thing was too close to the side of my
head for me to see the expression on its face.

But I could feel it wobbling from side to
side on my shoulder, which I decided meant
it was imagining that room as *hard* as it
could.

'– and *now* try to picture lots of kids like
me and Jackson in the water, splashing
around and having a good time!'

There.

I was pretty sure I'd done an excellent job
of explaining the Dolphin Leisure Centre
and Ali's party in a short and easy-to-
understand way.

Till I felt a wet nose nuzzling *right* inside my ear.

'Ooh! This place nice and *warm*, Rubby!' Thing mumbled at alarmingly close range.

Yuck!

As I made a grab for Thing, I spun around and saw Jackson crumpled up on the ground, half-laughing and half-choking on yet another jelly baby.

Sigh.

I am friends with a boy who is a donut
and a creature who sniffs ears for fun.
Am I the *only* sensible one around here …?

Strange eeks
and squeaks

YES!

That's the answer to the question on the last page.

I *know* I'm sensible because my teacher Miss Wilson says so. I'm always getting merits for having my homework in on time, remembering my PE kit and offering to sharpen the class pencils when they're not pointy.

My mum and dad tell me I'm sensible

too. Even as a tiny kid I'd fasten my seatbelt straightaway and eat all my vegetables – even the disgusting ones – without whining.

And I was sensible (again) after tea that evening.

Mum was washing the dishes and I was drying them, when I spotted an accident about to happen.

'Look out!' I yelped.

Mum had been gazing out of the window, and hadn't noticed a wet plate about to slither off the edge of the draining board.

'Ooh, good catch, Ruby!' gasped Mum. 'You really are *so* sensible, aren't you?'

'Mmmm,' I mumbled, picking up the checked tea towel and carrying on with my drying.

I realised that Mum might not say that if she knew I was hiding a mystery Thing at the bottom of the garden.

Just as well she had no idea what was
lurking in the trees ...

'Have you and Jackson made yourselves a
nice den out there?' Mum asked, gazing out
of the open window again.

'Sort of,' I said with a casual shrug.

'Your dad was just saying earlier that we
should sneak a peek at your secret world!'

Eek!

Suddenly, I felt as quivery as lemon jelly

with squirty cream on top.

I was frantically thinking what to say when Mum spoke again.

'Hey, *listen*. Can you hear a noise, Ruby?' she said, tilting her head.

Um, I could hear Dad clattering about in the distance, putting the rubbish and the recycling out by the front door.

But Mum didn't mean *that*, I was pretty sure. Her eyes were scanning the garden, and the trees, and even the new houses you could glimpse beyond all the leafiness.

'There's a funny sort of *flapping* or *splashing* sound coming from out there,' Mum continued. 'Oh, dear . . . I *hope* Christine hasn't caught anything!'

Ha! Christine cat is so old and lazy that she couldn't even catch her spider-on-a-string toy if I dangled it right in front of her whiskers. (Not even if I balanced it right on her *nose*.)

Nope, I was pretty sure the local wildlife was totally safe from our moggy.

But I did think I MIGHT know what was out there, flit-flapping and splish-sploshing.

'I'll go and check,' I said, stuffing the tea towel into the back pocket of my jeans and heading out of the back door.

Certain Mum was watching, I dillied and dallied, pretending to look here and there for signs of the strange eeks and squeaks.

All the while, I was deliberately meandering my way through our tangled garden, towards the overgrown rhododendron bush.

'Cause tucked out of sight behind its big, green bushiness was the stone birdbath.

Splish!

Splash!

Flit!

Flap!

'Wheeeee!'

'Thing!!' I hissed, spotting a familiar furry lump. 'What are you doing?!'

'I *zwimmin*, Rubby!' Thing purred happily, jumping up and down in the water. 'It *nice*!'

'It might be *nice*, Thing!' I hissed some

more. 'But do you have to be so *noisy*? What if my mum or dad had come to see what was going on?'

'Oh. Maybe I stay very, *very* still, Rubby?

Very, very, very, very, *very* still, so they not see me?'

Thing froze, like a small, extremely freaky statue. One that *no one* could miss in a million years.

Then I noticed that the statue was *shivering*.

'C'mere,' I said more gently, and scooped a soggy Thing out of the birdbath.

'Brrrrrr. This water not like *rain*, Rubby,' Thing muttered, cuddling up to my chest and soaking my T-shirt clean through. 'Rain run *off* me. *This* water too wet. It go inside my *furs*!'

I suddenly remembered the tea towel stuck in my back pocket and pulled it out.

In a blur, I began to frantically rub Thing dry. I couldn't risk it coming down with a serious case of the sneezles. I mean, it's not as if I could take it to the vet if it got ill, is it?

'OO-oo-OO-oo-OO!'

Yikes! I was so busy stressing that I was practically rubbing the damp fur clean off Thing.

'Sorry! But *shhh*!' I muttered, worried that Mum might hear.

'RUBY!!'

Yikes! (Again!) That was Mum! *Had* she heard?!

'EVERYTHING OK OUT THERE?'

I stuck my head around the side of the rhododendron bush.

'UH-HUH!' I called back, anxious that she stayed right where she was in the kitchen doorway. 'EVERYTHING'S FINE! IT WAS JUST A LITTLE ...'

My brain scrabbled about for a suitable lie.

'. . . SQUIRREL!' I finally blurted out.

Now, my answer might have sounded
sensible to *Mum*, but it didn't exactly impress
Thing.

After all, Thing couldn't stand . . .

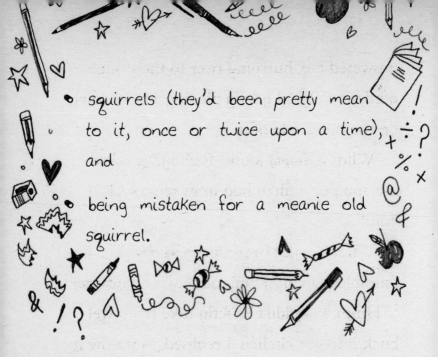

- squirrels (they'd been pretty mean to it, once or twice upon a time), and

- being mistaken for a meanie old squirrel.

'I is *NOT*—' Thing began to protest, but stopped dead when I pinched its snout shut.

'Shhh!' I whispered into its squirrelly little ears. 'I'm *trying* to get you back home, safe and sound!'

'OK, SWEETIE!' Mum's voice drifted towards me. 'BUT HURRY BACK – YOU'RE STILL ON DRYING DUTY, REMEMBER!!'

'ER . . . I'LL BE THERE IN A SEC!' I

answered her, hurrying over to the stone garden wall and gently placing Thing down on the other side of it.

'What is *drying* jootie, Rubby?' it asked me, snug as a furry bug in its tea towel bundle.

'What *I've* just been doing to *you*,' I mumbled, giving Thing one last rub all over.

Hmm. I couldn't exactly take the towel back into the kitchen, I realised. Not now it was covered in fluffy red hairs.

'You can keep that for tonight,' I whispered. 'Now curl up in your bed and get cosy.'

With its big saucer eyes blinking up at me, Thing looked incredibly sweet and snuggle-able.

I blew it a kiss (which confused it) and hurried away, before I did something silly, like pick it up and try to smuggle it to my room.

'See you soon!' I whispered softly behind me as I went.

But you know something?

I had NO idea just how soon 'soon' was going to be ...

Surprise, small surprise!

Spread out on my bed was a river, a waterfall, a swimming pool, a fountain and a sea.

(Christine cat was *also* spread out on my bed, with her snoring head lolling in the fountain and her tail lazily flicking in the Mediterranean.)

They were all images I'd printed out from the computer – except for Christine cat, who was too furry and fat to fit down a computer cable.

So what were all these print-outs for?

For Thing, of course.

I wanted to show it that water came in *lots* more ways besides rain and puddles.

After I'd finished drying the dishes with Mum, I got straight on the internet and researched these pictures, quicketty-quick.

In the morning, I'd look for a notebook and glue stick, so that I could present Thing with this, er, present after school.

But right now I was in the mood to be lazy and lie in a *different* kind of water – a bubbly, deep bath.

Actually, I reminded myself, I should go and check that it wasn't overflow—

SPLAT!

Glancing at my window, I saw a gloopy wodge of tissue stuck to the glass.

Only *one* person could land a perfect splat like that.

The sort of person whose bedroom was at
the side of their house, directly overlooking
mine.

I stomped to the window and flung it
open.

'Jackson!' I hissed, as – yuck! – the gloopy
wodge now slid down the pane and flumped

into the leaves of the wisteria that clung to the side of the cottage.

'Yes?' I heard my friend's voice say innocently.

'*That*', I growled, 'better *not* have been toilet paper!'

'*Might* have been!' Jackson said with a wide, dumb grin.

He was standing at his window, staring at me through a set of lookalike binoculars made out of loo-roll tubes and a bit of elastic.

'You are *so* annoying!' I told him.

'I am so *bored*, you mean!' he answered, using a longer kitchen-roll tube as megaphone. 'What are *you* up to, Ruby?'

'I've been printing something,' I replied.

'Yeah? Like what?' Jackson boomed at me.

'I'm doing a *project* on *water*, for *school*,' I said, while tilting my head in the direction

of the back garden,
and Thing.

Surely Jackson
would understand I
was talking in code,
in case of random
passing parents?

But of course, he
didn't.

'*What* project on water for school?!'

Sighing, I ran and scooped up the A4
sheets from the bed, and waved them at
Jackson.

'I mean, this is the sort of THING', I said,
tilting my head towards the garden again,
'that someone interested in *water* might like
to see!'

Jackson pointed his binoculars at the
print-outs and then at me.

'Why's your head twitching, Ruby?'

ARRGHH!

'There's noTHING wrong with my head!!' I barked at him.

'*And* you're speaking funny. You're freaking me out!' he yelled through his makeshift megaphone.

If there wasn't such a distance between us, I'd've been tempted to reach over and strangle Jackson Miller with my bare hands.

Instead, I did something *else* with them.

Letting the print-outs flutter to the floor, I held my hands to my chest like floppy paws and made my eyes as wide and as worried-looking as possible.

It was a pretty good impersonation of you-know-who, I was sure.

'Ah! Yeah! OK! So the pictures are for Th— *school*!!' gasped Jackson, getting my drift at long last. 'That's a brilliant idea! It —

I mean *school*, will love them! Actually, wait a minute . . . !!'

With that, Jackson and his toilet-roll tubes disappeared.

Tick-tock-tick, a minute or two passed by.

I guessed he must have gone to get something incredibly important to show me.

Tick-tock-tick, went another couple of minutes.

Or maybe he'd just gone to the loo.

Tick-tock-tick!

In the meantime, I listened to the rustle and swish of leaves in the evening breeze.

'Is you *lost* this, Rubby?'

I nearly jumped out of my freckly skin as a small surprise appeared on the window ledge.

So the rustles and swishes hadn't been caused by any breezy breezes – it had only been Thing scurrying up through the wisteria.

'Wow – were you *trying* to give me a shock?' I gasped.

'No, thank you,' said Thing, gazing up at me with a sweet, puzzled smile. 'I coming to *visit*, then found *this* . . .'

I looked down at its outstretched paw and saw a gloopy mush of toilet paper.

'Urgh!!' I muttered, taking hold of the mush with the smallest pinch of my fingers and lobbing it into the bin by my desk. 'So why did you want to visit me right now, Thing?'

'All *warm* now, Rubby. Not *need* this wrappings.'

Thing held up its *other* paw and offered me a muddy-looking piece of cloth with leaves and twiglets snarled into it.

'Uh, thank you,' I said, not much happier to take the tatty tea towel than the toilet-paper gloop. It could stay in the bin for now too . . .

'Actually, I have something for *you*,' I told
Thing, reaching down to the floor for the
print-outs. 'I was going to show you these
tomorrow, but since you're here . . .'

'Hey! Hi!' came a loud interruption from
the other window.

Jackson – grinning his best big baboon
grin – was gazing over at us, holding a

print-out of his own. (So *that's* what he'd been off doing.)

Thing scuttled round to face him, then stopped and stared hard.

Its stumpy wings wibbled and it began rocking from side to side – a sure sign it was confused.

Perhaps it was because Jackson had two cardboard horns growing out of his forehead. (He must've shoved his binoculars up there, out of the way, while he was on his computer.)

Or maybe it was because of the bright green cartoon creature visible on the white sheet of paper.

'Big caterpillar

is *zwimmin*, Rubby?' asked Thing, pointing at the wiggly shape.

'Ha!' snickered Jackson. 'I googled Loch Ness! This is the monster that *lives* in the loch!!'

Thing blinked, understanding just about *nothing* of what Jackson had said.

It turned and blinked up at me.

'Monsterer is *name* of big caterpillar, Rubby?' it purred hopefully.

Uh-oh.

'Well, the Loch Ness Monster is supposed to be a *little* bit bigger than a caterpillar,' I said gently, so I didn't alarm it.

'You're JOKING, *right*?' bellowed Jackson, with a laugh as loud as a small explosion. 'The Loch Ness Monster is as *huge* as Ruby's HOUSE! And MY house probably, put *together*!!'

'Is that right, Jackson?' I suddenly heard my mum's voice exclaim.

I whipped round and saw her standing in my bedroom doorway, smiling.

How *long* had she been there?

What had she *seen*?

The answers to those two questions had to be 'not very' and 'not much', or there was no *way* she'd be smiling . . .

'Um, hi, Mrs Morgan!' mumbled Jackson, wiggling his fingers in a limp and nervous hello.

'Hi, Jackson! It's a bit late for a conversation this lively, isn't it? How about saving it for the morning, for the walk to school?' Mum suggested, while waving back in Jackson's direction. 'And anyway, Ruby, I've just checked and your bath's ready . . .'

'OK!' I squawked, as my brain yelled, 'She must need glasses, *badly*!'

I mean, how *else* could Mum miss the weird and wonderful thing that was sitting on the sill?

'You know, the water was right at the top!' Mum said over her shoulder, as she walked away, back downstairs to Dad and the telly and normality. 'Just as well I noticed!'

'Thanks!' I called after her, finally daring to . . .

- breathe, and
- glance down at what she hadn't noticed.

What I saw was a small, extremely freaky statue staring back up at me.

'It's all right, she's gone,' I murmured.

'I stay very, *very* still, Rubby,' Thing purred up at me in a tiny, frightened voice. 'I stay very, very, very, very, *very* still, so she not *see* me . . .'

'Well done,' I said, patting it on its stumpy-winged back.

But it wasn't the statue impersonation that had saved us both; it was the Amazon River.

At least the *print-out* of the river that I'd been holding up in front of Thing the whole time, without even realising.

Who knew such a faraway splosh of water could be so useful?

'Hey, is everything OK?' came a husky boom, which I supposed was Jackson's pathetic attempt at a whisper.

'Yes!' I said sharply, closing the window on Jackson.

And his stupid cardboard megaphone.

And his stupid loo-roll horns.

And *especially* his stupid Loch Ness monster, which had nearly got us all caught.

'You like I *stay*, Rubby?' purred Thing, suddenly spotting (even if *I* hadn't) that closing the window meant I'd shut it inside.

I mulled for a second.

(An X-ray of my head would have shown the words 'good idea' and 'bad idea' swirling around at top speed.)

Then I nodded.

'Why not?' I announced, reckoning that Thing could *just* about fit in my dressing-gown pocket . . .

Beware the bubble fog . . .

'So, so *many* ubblies!' purred Thing in wonder.

'*Bubbles*,' I corrected it.

This wasn't the most relaxing bath I'd ever had.

Thing was finding the bathroom and all its sights and smells ridiculously exciting, and couldn't sit still.

Amongst other things, it had knocked the shampoo and conditioner bottles over and sent them skittling across the floor.

It had emptied an entire jar of cotton buds into the loo.

It had unravelled the toilet roll till it lay on the floor like a floppy, lopsided pyramid of paper.

'Look!' I said, scooping up some bubbles and blowing them into the air. 'You can make them *fly*!'

Yes, you guessed. I was just trying to distract Thing so it would take a break from *wrecking* stuff.

'Oooh!' cooed Thing, from its vantage point on the mixer tap.

It leant forward to grab a bubble or two – using the bath chain for balance – then jerked in panic at the sudden sound of gurgling.

'It's the plug! You've pulled it out *again*!' I explained, quickly thrashing around so I

could stop the warm water from vanishing.

'Ah . . . *not* pull plug,' it muttered, straightening up. 'I remember now, Rubby! Like *not* play with cloudy powder.'

'No. Talc *can* get a bit messy,' I agreed, looking at the whitish fur on top of Thing's head and thinking that I hadn't quite patted all of it out.

What Thing needed was a good wash.

Which meant it was in *exactly* the right place.

All I needed to do was coax it in . . .

'Why don't you give it a try?' I asked, making a splash or two to show Thing what fun bathwater could be. 'It's warm, I promise! Not chilly like the birdbath. And I'd make sure you were properly dry before you went back to your den!'

(I wasn't sure what Thing would make of the hairdryer, though – I'd have to explain

about the loud,
hot wind first . . .)

'Too *much*
water, Rubby,'
said Thing
uneasily, hopping from one foot
to the other, and hopping faster
when it put a foot on the hot
tap. 'Might be *monsterer* inside?'

Great. Instead of educating
Thing, Jackson had frightened
it, with tales of Loch Ness and
the non-existent big beastie
lurking in it.

'Honestly, there's only me and
some bubbles in here!' I tried to
reassure Thing.

'*Peh!*' it muttered,
unconvinced, before scampering
up the silver metal tubing coils

of the shower and swinging itself on to an unexplored shelf above the sink. 'What *this*?'

It picked up a pair of specs that Dad must have left there and held them up to examine.

I covered up a snigger with a soapy hand – gazing through the lenses, Thing's eyes loomed *twice* their size, like some 3D Disney character.

'Those are glasses. They help my dad to see clearly,' I told it, as straight-faced as I could.

'*Peh*! Make *you* all *fuzzy*!!' Thing grumped in disgust, dropping them back down in a

tangle of wire legs. 'And what *this* do? EEK!'

Who knew such a small creature could get into such huge pile of mischief so fast?

Not me, not till I met Thing . . .

'It's called shaving foam,' I explained, as I glanced around for my pink flannel, so I could wipe off the mousse that had just blobbed on to Dad's glasses. 'It's for—'

As I spoke, so did someone else, on the other side of the bathroom door.

'Hello in there!!' Dad called out brightly, as his knuckles interrupted with a tappitty-tap. 'Sorry to disturb you, Ruby, but I think I left my specs on the shelf when I had a shower earlier – mind if I grab them?'

'Um, OK!' I blurted out, quickly heaving myself up out of the water.

In a couple of soggy bounds, I could *grab* Dad's glasses, give them a *swipe* on the towel hanging from the radiator, and safely *slide* them out through a gap in the door only as wide as my hand.

So there would be NO chance of Dad catching sight of Thing.

Phew!!

'Thanks, honey!' said Dad, as the door suddenly opened wide.

NOOOOO!! I shrieked silently to myself, dive-bombing back into the bath and sending shock-waves splooshing over the sides.

The door!

I'd locked it!

Hadn't I?!

'I'm not looking, promise!' said Dad, holding a hand up to shield his eyes. 'I know young ladies need their privacy! Which is why I *must* get round to fixing this loose lock ...'

With the hand that *wasn't* shielding his eyes, Dad reached out towards the shelf.

The shelf where his specs were sitting, along with the tin of shaving foam, the beaker holding all our toothbrushes and toothpaste, and – thankfully – no Thing.

But wherever Thing was, it wasn't the *only* problem.

Please, please, PLEASE let Dad's hand hide the REST of the mess that Thing's made, I wished, keeping my fingers firmly crossed under the bubbles.

'Oops, how did this get here?' muttered Dad, scooping up his glasses and examining the foam-blob on the right-hand lens.

'How did what get *where*?' I mumbled, knowing how lame that must sound.

Dad must think I'd been goofing round with his stuff, making lotions and potions out of the bathroom products, like I did when I was a little kid.

'Never mind – it'll rub off,' Dad said

cheerfully, reversing back the way he'd come. 'I'll leave you in peace!'

Click went the door.

And *relaxxxxxx* . . . went my shoulders.

Dad hadn't seen Thing, *or* Thing's mess, which was all that mattered.

Now that we were out of danger, I glanced round the room for my little fuzzy friend – and saw a shivering, pink flannel by the edge of the bath.

'It's all right,' I tried to reassure Thing, as I lifted the cloth off its head. 'You did a great job of hiding, again!'

Two parents and two near misses in one evening – that *was* pretty nerve-racking. I needed to calm Thing down quick before . . .

Uh-oh.

Was it already too late?

White foam was frothing from its tiny mouth!!

Had it gone completely *mad* with panic?!

Ah, no…

I noticed the squeezed tube of toothpaste clutched in one paw and realised Thing had just had its first ever taste of mint – which didn't seem to have gone down too well.

'*Thish* NOT *niysh*, Rubby!' it jabbered, grabbing hold of its tongue. 'Inshide all *fizzzzzshly!*'

'Hold on – you need some water,' I told it quickly.

YUCK!

YUCK!

As I lunged for the tumbler by the sink, Thing did something *very* peculiar: it plunged headfirst into the bath.

'No! I didn't mean *that* kind of water!' I sighed, wishing I'd explained mouth-rinsing a bit better.

'EEEEEEEEKKKKK!!!'

OK, now we were in big, huge, GIANT trouble.

As Thing squeaked and splashed and did a good impression of drowning, I heard Dad's footsteps not very far away.

'You all right, Ruby?'

'YES!!! Just . . . just SINGING!!' I shouted out, absolutely desperate for him not to come back in. 'EEE-eeee-EEEEE!!'

'AARGHH!' gurgled Thing.

'AARGHH-*EEEEEE*-AARGHH!' I sing-songed.

'Mmm, nice tune!' I heard Dad laugh.

Then better still, I heard his footsteps fade away.

But help . . . grabbing Thing was like trying to grasp hold of a slippery soap, it was wriggling and squiggling and *drowning* so much.

Then at *last* I had it in my hands.

I was just lifting Thing to the safety of the bath's edge when I felt it shuddering in my grasp.

Uh-oh . . .

cRACKLE
sPIT
FIZZZZzZ!!

What was happening? (As if I didn't know!)

Flickers of light danced across the shiny tiles on the walls, as if someone had set off a sparkler.

Not *magic*! Not *here*! Not where my parents could find it, whatever it turned out to be!

The sparkles glittered and cartwheeled around the bathroom, bouncing off the mirror, the walls, the towel rail and the toilet seat.

Why had I been so stupid and shared my bathtime with Thing? I snapped at myself.

But then – just as soon as the mini fireworks show started – it *stopped*.

'Thing, what have you done?' I muttered, though it was a question that didn't really need an answer.

In fact, it was a slightly tricky question to ask.

With the bathroom completely filled
floor-to-ceiling with bubbles, talking
made me accidentally *swallow* some.

'Water make me go gah-gah-*gah*! So
I try to make it go *away*, Rubby!' Thing
answered, swizzling its arms around
like helicopter rotors and popping some
space. 'But it go wrong!'

Sigh.

Thing is as good at magic as I am at knitting with spaghetti, but it doesn't seem to have figured that out yet.

'Grab this . . .' I told it, letting go with one hand and feeling around for my flannel with the other.

'What we *do*, Rubby?' Thing squeaked, as I set it down on the side of the bath and pushed the pink cloth into its paws.

'We *flap*,' I ordered it, feeling round in the bubble-fog for my towel.

'Flap?' Thing quizzled, wafting its paws up and down. 'Like *birdie*?'

'Sort of. We flap and flap until ALL these bubbles have popped!'

Ten minutes later, I passed Mum in the corridor.

'Nice, chilled-out bath, Ruby?' she asked me.

'Yes,' I lied, as I kept my hand firmly over the bump in my dressing-gown pocket.

Chilled-out?

Ha!

I was so tired from frantic flapping and mess-fixing that I reckoned I could sleep till next Tuesday ...

Zip it!

Friday, 10 a.m.

Every week at this time, our class has swimming lessons at the Dolphin Leisure Centre pool.

Friday, 9.55 a.m.

Five minutes before our lesson *starts*, you'll find us all sitting shivering in our swimming costumes on the benches around the pool, waiting for our instructor (in his warm tracksuit) to turn up.

Today was Friday, it was 9.55, and I was a bit grumpy because I was ...

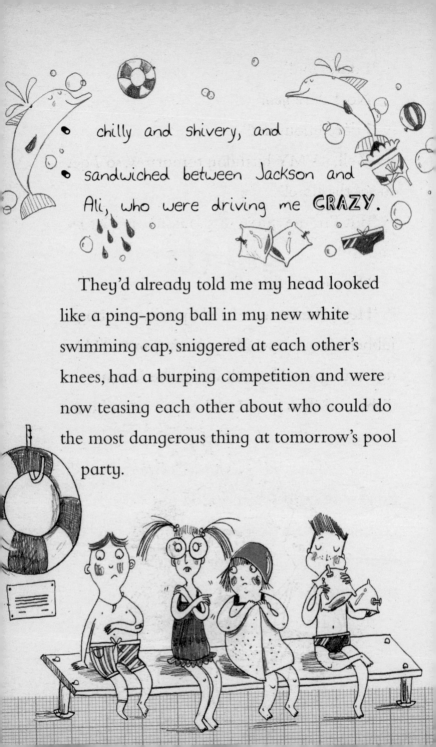

chilly and shivery, and

sandwiched between Jackson and Ali, who were driving me **CRAZY.**

They'd already told me my head looked like a ping-pong ball in my new white swimming cap, sniggered at each other's knees, had a burping competition and were now teasing each other about who could do the most dangerous thing at tomorrow's pool party.

'I dare you!'

'No, I dare *you*!'

'I dared you first!'

'Well, it's MY birthday tomorrow, so *I* get to set the dare!'

'But I'm the guest, so shouldn't you let *me* choose?'

'How is *that* fair?'

'Hey!' I interrupted, fed up with the boys jabbering over me. 'Why don't you BOTH agree to go backwards down the Mega-Tube and then you *don't* have to talk about it any more!'

I was pointing at the tallest of the three twirly slides when our teacher Miss Wilson appeared in front of me.

'NOBODY should be talking about ANYTHING right now, including *you*, Ruby!' she said, raising her eyebrows at me in a I'm-disappointed-in-you kind of way.

'But Miss Wil—' I began to protest, hoping she would see I was being Little Miss Sensible as usual, and it was the *boys* who were goofing around.

'Shhh!' Miss Wilson quietened me with a finger held to her lips. 'Mr Russo is here, so it's time to pay attention!'

Humff!

It was *so* unfair, being told off for something that wasn't my fault AND blushing bright pink from the tip of my toes to the tip of my nose.

I slouched down, arms tight-crossed, in a

fug of gloom . . .

'Did you hear that?' whispered Jackson, nudging me hard in the ribs.

'Ouch!' I mumbled, shooting him a sideways glower.

Yes, Mr Russo the instructor had been talking, but I hadn't been listening.

(I'd been too busy sulking and blushing.)

'He just said it's *vital* that *everyone* learns how to swim!!'

'So?' I mouthed.

Mr Russo *always* started off the lesson by saying something like that.

'Well, WE know someone who

can't swim, don't we?' Jackson whispered some more.

He meant Thing. I'd told him about last night's bathtime trauma on the way to school, while Dad dawdled behind, taking a call on his mobile.

'So?' I mouthed again.

What did Jackson want to do? Buy Thing a mini Speedo swimsuit and enrol it for lessons with Mr Russo?

'Well, you said yourself, Ruby, if you hadn't rescued Thing, it could've drowned!' he muttered urgently.

'Could we stop talking about this where people could hear, please?!' I suggested, just as urgently.

'Yeah, but Ruby,' Jackson carried right on, 'what if Thing fell into *another* type of deep water when neither of us was around?'

'*What* other type of deep water?'

'I dunno, do I? A . . . a raging river, or an abandoned well, maybe. Or a *whirlpool*!' Jackson babbled. 'I mean, what if it fell into

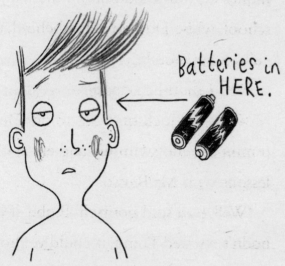

Batteries in HERE.

one of *those*, and couldn't swim?!'

I stared at Jackson, wondering if he needed new batteries for his brain.

It certainly didn't seem to be working properly.

Yeah, so he hadn't lived in our area for very long, but in case he hadn't noticed, our two houses were surrounded either by the

Forest View Homes estate or a whole bunch of farmers' fields.

There wasn't a raging river, abandoned well or whirlpool in *sight*.

I was just about to say so when someone noseyed in on our whispery conversation.

'Who are you guys talking about?' hissed Ali. '*Who* can't swim?'

'Just a friend of ours,' Jackson replied, giving me a nudge.

I could tell he thought I'd be impressed with him for inventing a cover-up, just like that.

But then he ruined it.

'It doesn't go to our school,' he said smugly.

'"*It*"?' repeated Ali, a confused frown untidying his forehead.

(*Wow*, was Jackson a dumb donut . . .)

'Excuse me, but what's all this chattering in aid of?' said Miss Wilson, suddenly

looming over us again, hands on hips.

Uh-oh.

We must've missed some instruction – the rest of the class were already up on their feet, ready to leap, slither or flop into the pool.

'Jackson and Ruby have a friend who can't swim, Miss!' announced Ali. 'That's terrible, isn't it, Miss?'

'Well, yes,' nodded Miss Wilson, sounding less cross now she thought we were talking about something important, rather than twirly slides and daft dares. 'Of *course* your friend should learn!'

'That's what I've been telling Ruby!' said Jackson.

Yikes – what was he *doing*?!

Miss Wilson might not know who (or *what*) Jackson was on about, but this was making me uneasy around the edges.

Staring hard at Jackson, I put my hand up to my mouth, and made a tiny 'zip-it!' sign.

Jackson either didn't notice, or pretended not to see it.

'Does your friend live nearby?' Miss Wilson continued. 'I'm sure there are lots of beginners' swimming courses here at the leisure centre . . .'

'Uh, *quite* near!' Jackson answered, giving me a quick wink.

I wished we were sitting at a table instead of on a bench so I could give him a kick under it.

'Cause the more he tried to be clever, the more chance there was of Jackson blurting out something he really, *really* shouldn't.

'Hey, you could bring your friend to my party, if you like!' Ali offered.

Jackson opened his mouth, but instead of something risky spilling *out* – *SPLOOOSH!!!* – a whole lot of chlorinated water rushed *in*.

'Oops, sorry!' I said quickly.

Fingers crossed that my deliberate *shove* had managed to look like an accidental *slip*.

Miss Wilson and Mr Russo seemed convinced – both of them grabbed an elbow to steady me.

But as Jackson popped up spluttering from under the water, I could tell *he* wasn't.

And he wasn't very pleased to hear everyone laughing at him.

Er . . . why *were* they laughing at him, exactly?

And what was that dark bit of cloth floating in the water?

ARRGHH!

The dark piece of cloth was someone's swim shorts, which must have come off when they dived (or were pushed) into the pool . . .

I flashed Jackson a look that I hoped said: 'Sorry, sorry, sorry! But you've *got* to stop talking about Thing – even in code!'

Yikes; here's the one he flashed me in return: 'I'm going to get you *back*, Ruby Morgan!'

It took until 10.57 a.m. that Friday morning to find out how exactly Jackson Miller planned to do that . . .

UN-fun with my UN-friend

It's always a rush getting dressed after swimming, isn't it?

That's why I didn't notice that both my school shoes were full of water till I put them on.

Can you imagine how uncomfy it was to walk back to school?

SQUELCH, *squish,* SQUELCH, *squish,* SQUELCH, *squish* . . .

Or wander round at lunchtime?

SQUELCH, *squish*, SQUELCH, *squish*, SQUELCH, *squish* . . .

Or go to the shops for Ali's birthday present after school?

SQUELCH, *squish*, SQUELCH, *squish*, SQUELCH, *squish* . . .

'Kick them off, honey, and I'll get them dry for the morning,' said Mum, as soon as we got back to our cottage, after the shopping trip.

I'd told her that it was an accident; that someone must've wrung out their swimsuit over my shoes without noticing.

'But why didn't you tell your mum the truth?' you might ask. 'Why didn't you blame Jackson for your poor, damp, prune-wrinkly tootsies?'

Well, of course I *wanted* to.

But how could I?

If I told Mum, she might have tutted at Jackson, and asked him why he'd acted like a big baboon.

Then Jackson would've told her it's 'cause I sent him flying into the swimming pool.

Which would've meant Mum asking me why I'd done such an un-sensible thing in the first place.

And how could I answer *that*, since it involved a Top Secret Subject?

Speaking of Top Secret Subjects, I wanted to go down to the trees, and check that Jackson hadn't done anything *spectacularly* stupid, like invite Ali back to meet our fuzzy little friend . . .

Does that sound mad?

I wasn't so sure. After all, Jackson had spent the *whole* day hanging out with Ali, and blanking me.

The leisure centre foyer was when I first

noticed. The class was lining up, getting ready to go back to school. Hidden by everyone's chitter-chatter, I'd cornered Jackson, pointed to my feet and hissed 'What did you do *that* for?'

Instead of answering, he'd turned to Ali and said, 'Can you hear something? Like an annoying *buzzy* sort of sound?'

Well, right now I was feeling as spiky as a wasp, so Jackson Miller'd better watch out . . .

'I'm just going outside; see if Jackson's there,' I muttered, dropping my schoolbag and the present for Ali on the hall table.

'Sure – have fun!' Mum called distractedly, as she ambled off somewhere with my soggy shoes.

Fun? Ha! I was probably about to have a whole bunch of *un*-fun with my *un*-friend, I thought, as I peeled off my damp socks and chucked them in the washing machine, before heading out of the back door.

PAD, *pad*, PAD, *pad*, PAD, *pad* . . .

The day's sun had made the grass feel deliciously warm on my bare feet.

PAD, *pad*, PAD, *pad*, PAD, *pad* . . .

With every warm step, my bad mood faded, bit by bit.

PAD, *pad*, PAD, *pad*, PAD, *pad* . . .

And as the black clouds of grumpiness drifted away, I suddenly saw something very clearly . . .

At the bottom of next-door's garden, a slightly writhing length of hosepipe was snaking over the fence, disappearing into the tangle of trees.

Huh?

Actually, now that the all-day grumbling had gone quiet in my brain, I could *hear* something unexpected too . . .

A gurgle and a whoosh.

I hurried as fast as I could (which is

tricky when you're trying to look casual, in case parents are peeking out of the window).

'Jackson – *what* is going on?' I asked, once I got to the low stone wall at the bottom of my garden.

A blow-up toddler paddling pool was positioned between the tree roots. The end of the snaking hosepipe was writhing around in it, with a gurgle and a whoosh, filling it up.

Christine cat was sitting mesmerised, slapping the flow of water with a paw if the nozzle dared to flip up.

And Jackson? He was tapping a plastic picture with a stick.

He'd laminated and hung up the print-out of the wiggly, bright green, cartoon Loch Ness Monster.

And he was using a voice that was a lot like Mr Russo's.

'It's very, *very* important that you know

how to swim. And if you practise, you can be as good a swimmer as *this*!' he was telling Thing, who was perched on his lap.

Thing was half paying attention to Jackson, and half looking at me.

'Boy – Rubby *talking*, Boy!' it muttered, pointing a paw at me.

'So . . . are you ready to get in?' Jackson asked, as if he hadn't heard me *or* Thing.

'But Rubby *there*, Boy. See?' insisted Thing, slapping a paw on either side of Jackson's face and trying to turn it in my direction.

'Jackson!' I snapped. 'Are you crazy?! What if your dad spots that hosepipe? He could walk down the garden to see what was going on and then—'

'Excuse me, Thing,' Jackson interrupted loudly, releasing Thing's paws from his cheeks, 'could you tell Ruby that *ONE*, my dad is busy on the computer, working.'

Thing gazed in confusion at the single finger Jackson was holding up in front of his furry face.

'*TWO*, I'm going to move the hosepipe in a couple of minutes when the pool is full.'

Thing gave both the fingers Jackson was now holding up a wary lick.

'And *THREE*, that I am SICK OF HER BEING SO BOSSY AND KNOW-IT-ALL AND TREATING ME LIKE AN IDIOT!!'

Thing and I were both stunned into blinking silence.

Till Thing spoke first.

'Rubby,' it began, fixing its headlamp eyes on me, 'Boy say lots of blah–blah wordies. What is *yiddly-yot*?'

My head swirled.

For the second time today I felt like yelping 'THAT IS *SO* NOT FAIR!'

I mean, all I ever wanted was to make sure Thing was safe, right?

Then I heard Jackson mutter something that made me even madder…

'We can have a good time on our own, Thing. Just *ignore* her.'

Well!

I turned and marched my way back up

the garden, towards the house.

After all, who wanted to hang around here and listen to a yiddly-yot like Jackson Miller?!

Though it was hard to walk away from the little voice calling out to me.

'Rubby! Not *go*, Rubby!'

Gulp.

'Me want to genorrr you!'

Or maybe it wasn't *that* hard . . .

Dazzles and disappearing acts

I stared at myself in the mirror at the Dolphin Leisure Centre and realised I'd made a BIG MISTAKE.

That morning I'd told Mum about the boys taking the mickey out of my ping-pong ball head. So she lent me *her* old swimming cap, which I thought was very cute, 'cause it was covered in flowers.

But now I was worried I looked a bit like
the rhododendron bush in my back garden.

'C'mon, Ruby! It's boys versus girls, and
we don't want them to beat us to the pool,
do we?!'

I wasn't sure which of the girls in my class
said that – they all zoomed by in a giggly
blur, burst through the swing door of the
changing rooms and were gone.

But I didn't feel much like zooming or
giggling or beating boys to the pool.

In fact, I didn't feel
much like being at Ali's
birthday party.

The truth is, I was
miserable, with a capital
'M'.

And a capital 'I', 'S',
'E', 'R', 'A', 'B', 'L' and 'E'
too.

I hadn't been able to sleep last night, I was so tossy-turny with hurt and grumpiness.

Jackson thought I was a bossy know-it-all, and Thing was happy to ignore me.

How rubbish was that?

As for this morning . . . In a huff, I thought I might leave for Ali's party without Jackson, just to punish him. Then Dad said he'd seen *Jackson* setting off without *me*!!

I guess *now* you might understand why I wasn't in a big hurry to see my un-friend here, or anywhere else, for that matter.

Still, I couldn't exactly get dressed and disappear, not when Ali had been nice enough to invite me.

As yuck as I felt, I had to get my bushy-head out to the pool and pretend to have fun.

I tugged open the swing door of the Female Changing Room – and suddenly saw the *strangest* sight, right across the corridor…

FLIP! went the door to the Male Changing Room, as a dad and his kid in Day-Glo armbands came out.

FLAP! The door swung inwards again, giving me a glimpse of Jackson, on his knees, *knocking* on a locker door!

FLIP! I crossed the corridor, grabbed the Male Changing Room door on the out-swing, and stared.

But my un-friend wasn't just knocking on the locker door – he was *talking* to it!

Wow, whoever heard of someone having a conversation with a leisure-centre locker before?

Unless . . .

Uh-oh.

'Please, *please* come out!' I heard Jackson say to the grey, grilled metal door.

'Oi!' I whispered, glancing from left to right, on the look-out for boys in their

boxer shorts who might shout at me to get
out. (Luckily, there were no boys – or boxer
shorts – in sight.)

At the sound of my voice, Jackson's
head whipped round. A look of pure relief
appeared on his face.

Hurray – he'd forgotten to be cross with
me!

Possibly because he desperately needed my
help . . .

'Ruby! It's shut itself in, and I can't get it
to come out!'

'You're not talking about your shower gel,
are you?' I asked, scooting over to join him.
'What's going on?'

'Thing wanted to watch everyone
swimming, so it could get some tips!' he
explained. 'I even made it *this*, so it could sit
at the edge of the pool in disguise!'

He was holding up a Bart Simpson towel

and poking two fingers through a couple of holes he'd snipped in the cotton, exactly where Bart's eyes should be.

Skipping over the fact that Thing would look like a creepy cartoon ghost in that, I bent down and spoke directly to the locker.

'Thing – this is Ruby!' I said in a soft but stern voice. 'I'm going to count to ten, and I want you to come out. One—'

'Rubby!' Thing yelped in delight, immediately whacking the locker door open on to Jackson's fingers. (Ouch.)

PHREEEEEEEEPPPPPPP!!!!

I shot straight up, and found myself looking at a huge bloke in short shorts and a tight Dolphin Leisure Centre T-shirt, with a whistle around his neck.

'Oi, little girl! Female Changing Rooms over *there*! OK?' he bellowed, chucking a thumb behind him.

'OK!' I mumbled.

With that, the lifeguard gave a grunt and was gone, on his way to save lives or blow his whistle at someone else doing something they shouldn't.

'Phew . . .' I sighed in relief, turning to face Jackson. 'Thank goodness he didn't see—'

I froze, as soon as I saw Jackson's face.

I could tell a complete disaster had happened.

Or *worse*.

'Thing panicked when it heard the

whistle, Ruby!' he said at high speed. 'It ran away – *that* way!'

That way?

That way led out to the foyer, and the front doors!

Heaps of people would be there, milling around or queuing to get in.

A small, skittering, wild-eyed Thing would stand out like a sardine in a box of chocolates!

I held my breath for a second, bracing myself to hear screaming – but there was just a distant hubbub of chit-chat.

Maybe we still had time?

'Come on,' I urged Jackson, shoving him, his bashed fingers and his terrible towel disguise towards the door at the far end of the changing room.

FLIP!

We were out in the main corridor, with

the foyer just beyond.

'Wait!' I told Jackson, pulling him out of sight behind a handy vending machine.

From here we could JUST about scan the foyer, AND hide the fact that we were only dressed in our swimmies.

'Dada! Want one!' a tiny girl was demanding, pointing at some sweets or crisps or yummy something in the machine.

'See anything?' whispered Jackson.

'Nope,' I replied, quite pleased to have the tiny girl and her uninterested Dad as cover, as well as the vending machine.

'Not now, Shannon,' the dad said flatly, as he carried on some separate conversation on his mobile.

'But, Dada, I want it! *Pleeeeaaasssse*!!'

'How about those chairs over there?' hissed Jackson, nodding his head towards a cluster of orange plastic seats, near the pay desks.

'Shannon, I said *no*!!' snapped the dad, phone still clamped to the side of his head.

'I'll check . . .' I mumbled to Jackson, sliding down on to my bare knees, so I could get a semi-decent, long-distance peek under the seats he'd pointed out.

'But I *want* it . . . it is so *cute*!' whined the tiny girl, squashing her hands and her button nose up against the glass.

Wait a minute.

Since when did anyone – even a tiddly little kid – call a chocolate bar or a packet of crisps 'cute'?

I turned my head a centimetre or two . . . and came face-to-face (through the sheet of glass) with something that *definitely* couldn't be described as a snack.

'Help!' Thing mouthed at me.

'Stop whinging, Shannon! Come *on*!!' ordered the dad, grabbing the tiny girl's

hand and dragging her away.

Her other hand stretched longingly behind
her, towards the ball of red fur hovering on
the rack reserved for Quavers.

With the corridor briefly empty of
witnesses, I flicked open the vending-
machine flap and mouthed 'Jump!' at Thing.

It jumped, and landed in the drawer

(along with a packet of Quavers it had accidentally dislodged).

I tugged the Bart Simpson towel out of Jackson's hands and quickly used it to bundle Thing up.

'What now?' asked Jackson, desperate for answers from *me*, his bossy, know-it-all friend. (Ha!)

'We get changed and we leave for home, as quick as we can!' I told him.

It wasn't a perfect plan.

We'd have to think of a good excuse to give Ali.

And our parents, who we'd have to phone to come and collect us early.

But we could worry about our excuses while we were getting dressed and—

'Jackson! Ruby! What are you two doing out here?' said a smiley woman carrying a huge birthday cake in the shape of a swimming pool with 'Happy Birthday, Ali' piped on the blue icing.

'We were . . . *thirsty!*' Jackson told Ali's mum, pointing at the vending machine.

It would have been a great excuse, except for the fact that there were no *drinks* in there.

'Don't you worry!' said Ali's mum, nodding at the man following laden with bags. 'Ali's dad's got bottles of water in that green carrier. Help yourself – then get inside and don't miss the fun. See you in the party room after!'

What could we do?

Not much except say thank you very nicely and head off towards the pool, clutching our drinks and our suspiciously lumpy roll of towel . . .

'Raaaaaaahhhhhh!'

'Wheeeeeeeeee!'

'Againagainagainagain!'

During the week, the Dolphin Leisure Centre pool is filled with schoolkids doing lessons and bobbing old ladies.

But at the weekends it's packed with shrieking children, roaring big-kid dads, dive-bombing teenagers and a zillion inflatables of every shape, size and weirdness.

There are long, chatty queues of people climbing the stairs that lead to the three twirly slides. And every few minutes, there's cheering as the wave machine starts up in the main pool, and the fast current comes on in the tiled corridor that's known as Typhoon Tunnel.

I worried that all this dazzle of noise and colour might stress Thing, so I held it close and snuggly.

'I'll just sit here at the edge, with the

"towel" on my lap,' I mumbled to Jackson, slipping into code-talk.

'Good idea. Well, I'll sit with you-ooo-*ahhhhh*!!'

Jackson was suddenly scooped up by the elbows and hurtled towards the stairs leading to the Mega-Tube (the scariest of the twirly slides) by a couple of boys from our class.

He glanced a 'sorry!' over his shoulder at me as I perched on the bench.

I gave him a shrug back.

It was probably better that Jackson joined in with the partying and acted normal, i.e. like a big baboon.

(If he didn't, people might get suspicious.)

If Ali or anyone asked *me* what I was doing, I'd say I had a headache, and I was going to stay here sipping water, till I felt better.

(They'd think that was just me, being super-sensible as usual.)

I settled the lumpy towel on my lap, and felt the scrabble of Thing's feet on my lap. And with a casual re-jiggle and tug, I got the snipped 'eye' holes facing my way.

'You *like*, Rubby?' purred a small voice, as a yellow curly crisp came poking out from under the towel.

'Don't! Someone will see!' I hissed, poking the Quaver back inside. 'And don't talk!'

No reply.

Good.

Thing was quiet.

For a few seconds at least.

'I not like it when you all frowny last night, Rubby!' the towel suddenly murmured.

Well, I didn't much like you saying you wanted to *ignore* me, I thought, but didn't say.

'Shhh!' I muttered, covering my mouth so it might look like I was coughing from a distance. 'Just keep quiet and I'll swizzle you around so you can see what's going on!'

Hurray – *that* worked.

Thing sat silent and still, swallowing up all the sights and sounds.

People laughing, as their lilos and rubber rings collided.

People whooping, as a klaxon sounded and the wave machine swayed into action.

People cheering, as the Typhoon Tunnel swept them through at top speed.

'RUUUUUBBBBEEEEEE!!!!!'

And that lung-busting yell came from Jackson (of course).

There he was, hurtling headfirst down the mighty Mega-Tube.

SPLOOOSH!

Jackson landed in the pool, causing an impressive tidal wave.

Wow . . . it was quite a steep drop at the end there.

Jackson seemed to be taking a long time to surface.

A very *lonnnnnnnnnngg* time, actually.

'Rubby!' came an urgent small voice.

Scratchy small feet were padding side to side on my thighs.

'Shh!' I urged it, as I kept my eyes on the spot where Jackson would hopefully ping up any second.

'But where *Boy*?!' Thing purred worriedly. 'He be *drowned*-ing?'

'No – I'm sure he's fine,' I said, though I was starting to fret a little too.

In fact, I was fretting quite a LOT.

Fretting so much that I didn't at first notice the tell-tale tremble going on under the towel.

I did jump though, the minute I felt tickly prickles on my tummy.

Uh-oh . . .

Was *that* what a

cRACKLE
sPIT
FIZzZZZzzZ!!

felt like?

I lifted the edge of the towel, and saw a sparkle of light – then flipped it back down again quicketty-quick, before any colours came cartwheeling out.

'Thing! Stop!!' I urged it, though I knew it was too late.

Whatever magic spell Thing had cast, it had already happened.

And any second now, I'd probably figure out what trouble we were in . . .

Floop!

The towel collapsed, into an empty pile in my lap.

ARRGHH!

Where – in the whole of the noisy, splashy, crowded Dolphin Leisure Centre – had Thing disappeared to . . . ?!

Magic (and trouble) x 2

'Whoo-hooo!! Did you see that dive I took at the end, Ruby?' asked Jackson, breathless and pulling himself out of the water.

It was great that he was . . .

- alive, and

- having fun.

It was *also* great that he seemed to have forgotten the bad feeling between us.

He wasn't going to feel so great in a second, though, not once I'd told him what had just happened . . .

'Jackson – Thing's vanished!' I said, as I helped haul him up on to the pool-side.

'Huh?' he gasped, flopping down beside me like a fish in swim shorts.

'It thought you were drowned-ing – I mean *drowning*. I think it tried to do some magic that would save you!' I muttered, scanning the packed pool at the same time.

'But how?' Jackson asked uselessly.

'I don't know, do I? One minute it was under Bart Simpson, the next it wasn't. I had to hide the towel behind the bench, so no one saw the sparkles leaking out . . .'

Help – the pool was WAY too crowded with people and blow-up balls and lolloping lilos to BEGIN to spot Thing.

And for all we knew, it could be on the roof of the building, or halfway down the Mega-Tube, or back in the vending machine.

How on earth were we supposed to find our freaky friend?!?

'Er . . .' I heard Jackson mumble.

He was pointing at a plastic ball that was twirling on the surface of the water.

It was coming straight for his knees.

Through the see-through coloured panels, you could JUST make out a little, bug-eyed creature running madly inside . . .

THING!

Me and Jackson turned to each other, then slid into the pool like a pair of synchronised swimmers.

'Ruby, some kid is going to come looking for this!' said Jackson, as we both slapped our wet hands on the ball.

'I know – so let's push it towards the Typhoon Tunnel,' I suggested. 'We'll be more hidden away there!'

Like the wave machine out in the main pool, the current in the tunnel was currently switched off. No one much would use the semi-circle of tunnel till the klaxon sounded and the water went wibbly and wild again.

Together we splashed and swam, while Thing scampered like a hyper-active hamster in an oversized exercise ball.

And finally we were there, in the white-tiled safety of the tunnel.

Gasp!

(Oops, I'd forgotten to breathe.)

Standing chest-high in the water, I gulped air and left Jackson to find out what had gone wrong, oh-so-wrong.

'Hey, what just happened?' he asked Thing, his mouth a millimetre from the plastic.

Tilting his head, Jackson pressed his ear up against the ball to hear the reply.

Inside, I could see Thing's tiny mouth

frantically babbling an explanation.

'It tried to magic up a rubber ring to rescue me!' Jackson translated. 'But instead it ended up stuck inside *this*!'

'Well, we'll have to get it out of there,' I said, reaching over and unpopping the stopper at the side. 'We can hide this in your bag while we're eating cake with Ali, and then we'll cut Thing out once we get home.'

Pssssssssssffffffffhhhhh!

'But it's like we're stealing some kid's toy!' said Jackson, staring at the gently deflating ball.

'Yeah, but we can hardly hand it back with Thing inside, can we?' I pointed out.

'I guess. OK, I'll tell it what's happening,' said Jackson, and went to put his mouth back against the rapidly wrinkling plastic.

No words came out, though.

Not when he caught sight of the terrified

expression on Thing's face.

What was it staring at?

We both followed Thing's panicked gaze, and saw . . .

Dun-*dun*-DUN!!

. . . an escaped lilo come gently bobbling and swaying into the tunnel.

It was green, with a blow-up head on the front that you could hang on to. (Not that anyone was hanging on to it – it had obviously floated away from its owner when they were busy dive-bombing or Mega-tubing or in the loos.)

The cartoony head had cross-eyes and a goofy smile.

It was so cute and dopey-looking that no one in the entire history of the universe could *ever* think it was frightening in any way.

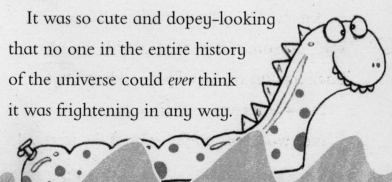

Unless you were called Thing, of course.

'Monsterer!' I saw it mouth inside the ball.

CRACKLE
SPIT
FIZZZZzzZ!!

No!

Not AGAIN!

Flickers of light filled the deflating inflatable ball, as if Thing was wafting a sparkler inside.

HISS! FNIIINNGGG!!

A tiny fountain of light sprang out of the stopper, turning into a cartwheel of spangles that bounced over the lapping water.

But as soon as this mini fireworks show started, it stopped.

Wow.

How incredibly lucky was it that only me and Jackson saw that?

Oh.

AND the six-year-old boy who'd just

come doggy-paddling into the tunnel after
his lost lilo.

A lost lilo, which had *just* that second
turned into something it really *shouldn't* have.

'Um . . . is that the Loch Ness Monster, do
you think?' asked Jackson, as the lilo swelled,
doubled and *trebled* in size, and its six-year-old
owner went silent and wide-eyed with shock.

'Yep,' I nodded, watching as the lilo turned
into a hump-backed monster, and wishing
my legs hadn't just turned to noodles.

So, Thing had magicked up a giant,

fearsome, living, breathing creature.

Could it get any worse?

Oh, yes.

PAAAAARRRRPPPPP!!!

The klaxon blasted and the current
instantly got stronger in Typhoon Tunnel.

'EEEEEEEE!!' screamed the boy.

'NOOOO!!' yelped me and Jackson.

'YAY!!' called a bunch of voices, as people
began rushing towards the tunnel.

'AARGHH!!' came a weeny screech from
inside the deflating ball, as the Loch Ness

Lilo reared its rapidly growing head out of the water and . . .

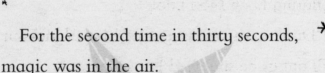

CRACKLE
SPIT
FIZZZZzzZ!!

For the second time in thirty seconds, magic was in the air.

Once again, sparkles poured out of the tiny opening of the stopper like a fountain of light, and went cartwheeling off the sides of the tunnel.

'*Please* fix this, Thing!' I muttered to myself, hoping that Ali didn't end up with a birthday party he'd never forget. (One where the Loch Ness Lilo oozed around, devouring random Dolphin Leisure Centre customers . . .)

Then, just as soon as this mini fireworks show started, it stopped.

What *hadn't* stopped was the current of water now picking us up and hurtling me, Jackson and Thing towards the other end of the tunnel . . .

But Thing wasn't inside the deflating plastic ball any more – it was on *top* of a deflating Loch Ness Lilo!

'Don't worry – I've got it!' I heard Jackson call out as he snatched Thing to safety.

Out in the main pool, I struggled in the waves to get myself the right way round and see what had happened.

Finding my feet at last, I caught a glimpse of a stunned-looking six-year-old being swept out of the tunnel on the crest of a mini-wave, with a limp, deflated green lilo clutched in one white-knuckled fist.

Just *wait* till his family heard his story!

They were never going to believe it. And I mean, *never*.

(Thank goodness . . .)

'Changing Room, *now*!' I said, grabbing a passing stray float to shield Thing with.

'Yes, boss!' Jackson answered happily, taking it from me.

Even in the muddle of the panic, I couldn't help smiling at his words . . .

Bye-bye, you-know-what!

It was Saturday afternoon, about half-past four, and it was time for quite a lot of sorries.

Oh, and cake.

'Sorry it's a bit squashed,' said Jackson, unfolding the serviette on the scrubby ground and presenting Thing with a section of Ali's birthday cake.

(The squished brown icing was a bit of the swimming lessons bench, I was pretty sure.)

Thing gave it a sniff, and pulled a yuck-
face.

'No, thank you,' it purred, and went back
to nervously nibbling on the dead daisy chain,
the one I'd hung around the back door of its
Scooby-Doo den earlier in the week.

I looked up from what I was doing
(swapping swimming caps round – I
reckoned I preferred having a red head to an
egg-head or bush-head).

'What's wrong, Thing?' I asked, glancing

up from fitting the white rubber over the trampoline tin. 'You're home, sweet home!'

Thing looked as squished as the icing, but I guess that's what happens when you're stuck inside a sweaty sports hold-all for the whole of a party.

'*Peh*,' muttered Thing, now scrambling inside the Mystery Machine van, and sitting with its furry back to us.

Jackson – who'd started eating the cake since it was going spare – frowned at me.

'Maybe I could cheer it up?' he mumbled with his mouth full, while grabbing a can of Coke he'd nabbed from the party. 'I could burp a song it liked!'

Of course a suggestion like that *deserved* to be ignored, so that's what I did.

'Thing,' I said softly, getting down on my hands and knees so my face was at van-level. '*Please* tell us what's wrong!'

'Not like monsterer *looking* at me!' it mumbled.

'The print-out!' I said, straightening up and pointing to the laminated cartoon of the Loch Ness You-Know-What.

'Sorry, Thing!' said Jackson, reaching over and snatching the picture off the skinny branch with a twang. 'I didn't know it would frighten you so much. I just thought you'd think it was cool. But see – it's gone now!'

Thing swizzled round, with a wary peek at where the picture wasn't.

'And *I* sorry,' it purred, rubbing its paws together, 'for troublings I make at poo party …'

DON'T I glowered at Jackson, before he burst out laughing.

'OK,' he said, swallowing his sniggers. 'If we're all saying sorry, then I want to say sorry I told you that your head looked like a ping-pong ball in swimming lessons, Ruby!'

'Oh! Thank you!' I said in surprise.

Jackson apologising for being a big baboon didn't happen very often. About as often as ducks go moo.

'Though it WAS better than the dumb flowery hat you had on today,' he added, annoyingly.

I huffed for a second, but knew he had a point. I didn't suit looking like a bush.

'And sorry I said you were a know-it-all, and all that stuff,' he added with a shrug. 'I guess you *are* kind of smart and sensible and whatever . . .'

It was a bit rambly, but I was still touched. Maybe it was time I added a sorry of my own?

'Well, *I'm* sorry if I ever sound bossy,' I told him.

As Jackson and I grinned at each other, Thing scuttled on to my lap, threw itself star-

shaped against my belly and squeezed me tight.

'Er, what are you doing?' I asked it.

'Rubby and Boy happy. *I* happy. So I *genorrr* you,' it purred so loudly it made my tummy rumble.

'Hold on; *this* is what you thought "ignoring" meant?' I asked, remembering that evening I marched all miserable and mumfy up the garden.

'It not *this*?' Thing purred in surprise.

'No! Ignoring means pretending someone isn't there,' I explained.

'Oh!' squeaked Thing. 'I thought it sound like *nice* word. Like a *huggy* word.'

'Hey, you me and Thing – let's ALL *genorrr* each other!' announced Jackson.

And with that, he threw his arms around us both in a big bear hug, which was kind of embarrassing and kind of, well, *nice*.

Me and Jackson, Jackson and
me.
And Thing, of course.
We'll never be un-friends
again . . .*

(* Yeah – same as Jackson will never be
annoying and Thing will never, ever do
a single *speck* more rubbish magic. In my
dreams!!)

YOu, me and Thing

KAREN mCCOMBIE

The **Curse** of the **Jelly Babies**

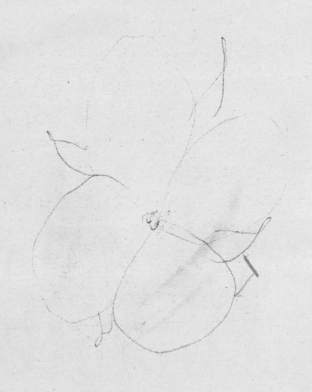